First published in Belgium and Holland by Clavis Uitgeverij, Hasselt – Amsterdam, 2015
Copyright © 2015, Clavis Uitgeverij

English translation from the Dutch by Clavis Publishing Inc. New York
Copyright © 2017 for the English language edition: Clavis Publishing Inc. New York

Visit us on the web at www.clavisbooks.com

Looking for Colors with Lily and Milo written and illustrated by Pauline Oud
Original title: *Kleurtjes zoeken met Fien en Milo*
Translated from the Dutch by Clavis Publishing

ISBN 978-1-60537-336-2

This book was printed in January 2017 at Wai Man Book Binding (China) Ltd. Flat A, 9/F., Phase 1,
Kwun Tong Industrial Centre, 472-484 Kwun Tong Road, Kwun Tong, Kowloon, H.K.

First Edition
10 9 8 7 6 5 4 3 2 1

Clavis Publishing supports the First Amendment and celebrates the right to read

Looking for Colors with
Lily and Milo

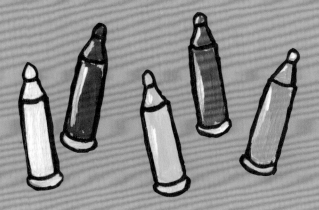

Clavis

Pauline Oud

Lily and Milo are going to play outside today.
They need their boots!
Lily and Milo are looking for their **red** boots.
Can you help them?

Found them! Lily and Milo are wearing their **red** boots.

They jump in a big puddle. How fun!
Oops... Lily is getting all wet!

Look, there is the sandbox.
Lily and Milo are going to dig a big hole!
They are looking for their **green** shovels.
Can you see them?

Found them! Lily and Milo are playing
in the sandbox with their **green** shovels.

Lily is digging a very deep hole.
And what is Milo doing? Oops....

"Look at that, Lily!"
Milo calls.
"Balloons!"

Lily and Milo both choose a pretty balloon.
What is the prettiest color? **"Yellow,"** Milo calls happily.
Lily and Milo both choose a **yellow** balloon.
But are there any **yellow** balloons? Do you see any?

Yes! Lily and Milo both have a **yellow** balloon.
Aren't they pretty?
"Be careful, Milo."
Bang! goes Milo's balloon suddenly.
"Don't cry, Milo," Lily says.
"You can have *my* balloon."

It's almost time to go home.
"Where is your cart?" Lily asks Milo.
Milo doesn't know. They look everywhere in the park.
"Over there!" he calls happily.
Milo's cart is **blue**. Do you see it anywhere?

Found it! Lily and Milo pull their **blue** cart home.
Milo gets to sit in the cart, because he is a little tired.
Oops! The balloon flies away!

"Don't cry, Milo," Lily says.
"Look, the balloon is happy
and flies towards
the **yellow** sun!"

Back at home, Lily and Milo are very thirsty.
What will they drink?
There is milk, lemonade with a straw,
a cup of coffee and **orange** juice.
Lily and Milo both choose a glass of **orange** juice.
Do you see the **orange** juice?

Yummy, it's delicious!
Lily drinks her **orange** juice in one go.
Milo wants to drink something too.

But oops! What is Milo doing now?

Now Lily and Milo want to make a nice drawing.
They both have a big piece of paper.
The paper is **white**.
In the big box there are **red, green, yellow,**
blue and **orange** felt-tip pens.
Can you find them all?

Lily's drawing is all done.
"Look, Milo!" she calls happily.
"I drew **red**, **yellow**, **green**,
blue and **orange** balloons!"

But oops.... What has Milo done now?

Which colors do Lily and Milo find?

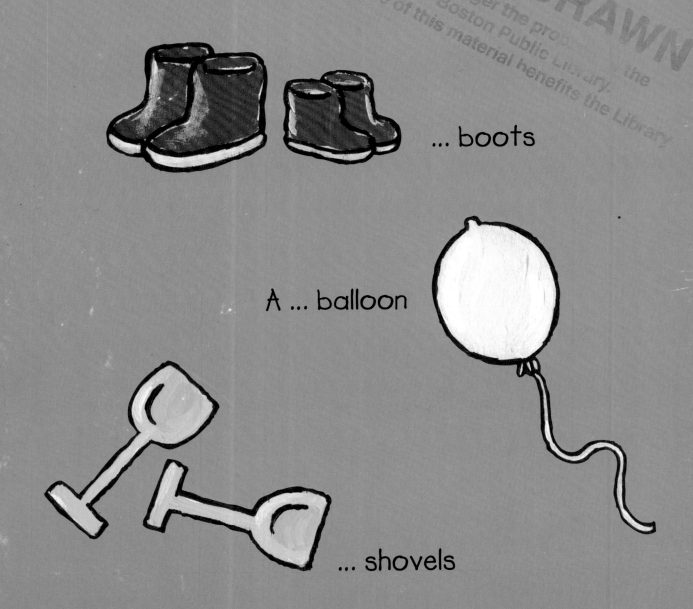

... boots

A ... balloon

... shovels